W9-BHG-811

Annie and Snowball and the Dress-up Birthday

The First Book of Their Adventures

Cynthia Rylant
Illustrated by Suçie Stevenson

SCHOLASTIC INC.

New York Toronto London Auckland Sydney
Mexico City New Delhi Hong Kong Buenos Aires

For Jane Stevenson
—S. S.

No part of this publication may be reproduced, stored in a retrieval system,
or transmitted in any form or by any means, electronic, mechanical, photocopying,
recording, or otherwise, without written permission of the publisher. For information
regarding permission, write to Simon & Schuster Books for Young Readers, Simon & Schuster
Children's Publishing Division, 1230 Avenue of the Americas, New York, NY 10020.

ISBN-13: 978-0-545-03714-3
ISBN-10: 0-545-03714-X

Text copyright © 2007 by Cynthia Rylant.
Illustrations copyright © 2007 by Suçie Stevenson.
All rights reserved. Published by Scholastic Inc., 557 Broadway, New York, NY 10012,
by arrangement with Simon & Schuster Books for Young Readers, Simon & Schuster Children's
Publishing Division. SCHOLASTIC and associated logos are trademarks
and/or registered trademarks of Scholastic Inc.

12 11 10 9 8 7 6 5 4 3 2 1   7 8 9 10 11 12/0

Printed in the U.S.A.   23

First Scholastic printing, September 2007

Book design by Jessica Sonkin

The text for this book is set in Goudy.

The illustrations for this book are rendered in pen-and-ink and watercolor.

Contents

Favorite Things

It was almost Annie's birthday,
and Annie was very excited.
On birthdays Annie got to wear
her favorite things:
ribbons and bows and lace
and fancy little shoes.

This year she had her new bunny,
Snowball.
She would dress up Snowball, too!
Annie couldn't wait.

Annie decided she wanted to celebrate
her birthday with just her family.
Her family was her dad and Snowball,
of course.

But Annie's family was
also her cousin Henry,
Henry's parents,
and Henry's big dog,
Mudge.

Annie had moved next door
to Henry and Mudge, and she loved it.

They watched old movies and
ate popcorn on Friday nights.
They threw Frisbees.
They played board games.

And, of course, Annie and Henry
spoiled each other's pets.
Annie adored Mudge.
She gave him good brushings.

And Henry liked Snowball.

He gave her good scratchings.

It was so much fun living side by side!

So Annie decided to have a nice, quiet
birthday with her family.
She'd ask everyone to dress up.
It would be great!

Dress-up Plans

Annie telephoned Henry.
Henry and Mudge were cleaning
Henry's fish tank.
Henry was cleaning, and Mudge
was handling the spills.

When Henry answered the phone,
Annie told him that Tuesday was
her birthday.

"Dad is going to make my favorite foods," said Annie.

"Finger sandwiches and lemon tarts and strawberries dipped in chocolate."

"Yum," said Henry, scrubbing his castle.
Mudge was wiping up the floor.

"And it's going to be
a Dress-up Birthday," said Annie.
"Great!" said Henry.
"Tell your parents, okay?" said Annie.
"Sure!" said Henry.
Annie and Henry said good-bye.

Annie imagined what she would wear
for her Dress-up Birthday.
And she couldn't wait to dress up
Snowball!

Next door Henry imagined
what he would wear.
And he couldn't wait to dress up
Mudge!
Annie's birthday would be fun!

A Happy Day

Tuesday came and Annie's house
looked beautiful.
Annie's dad had filled it with daisies
and carnations and yellow balloons.

Annie looked beautiful too.
She had dressed up in her best satin
dress and sparkly pink tights and little
white gloves with pearls.

Snowball also looked nice.
She had lacy ears and a glittery nose
and a little blue bow on her tail.

Even Annie's dad looked special.

He was in a tuxedo.

(Annie had asked.)

Finally the doorbell rang.
"That must be Henry!" said Annie.
Annie and Snowball and Annie's dad
opened the door.

And there stood a pirate, a gypsy,
a mummy, and a moose.
For a moment everybody just stared.

Then the pirate said to Annie,
"I thought you told me this was
a dress-up party."
"It is," said Annie.

"Well, I thought you meant costumes,"
the pirate said as one of the moose's
antlers fell off.

"Gee," said the mummy, "I did put on
my best bandages."
Everyone laughed and laughed.

34

Then they all had a lovely party.
The mummy served the tarts,
and the pretend moose
and the bunny cleaned
up the crumbs.

Annie got a new teacup,
a pretty doll,
and a special set
of little china plates.

Then when everything was finished,
the gypsy told everyone's fortunes.

She told Annie that all of Annie's days
would be as happy as this one.

But Annie already knew that.
Because she had Snowball
and Henry and Mudge
as her very best friends!